Appelard and Liverwurst

Appelard and Liverwurst

story by **MERCER MAYER**
pictures by **STEVEN KELLOGG**

MORROW JUNIOR BOOKS
NEW YORK

William Morrow and Company, Inc.,
105 Madison Avenue,
New York, NY 10016.
Printed in the United States of America.
1 2 3 4 5 6 7 8 9 10
Library of Congress Cataloging-in-Publication Data
Mayer, Mercer, 1943–
Appelard and Liverwurst / story by Mercer Mayer ; pictures by
Steven Kellogg.
p.   cm.
Summary: Aided by a wayward rhinoceros, Appelard and his motley
farm animals finally have a successful harvest.
ISBN 0-688-09659-X. —ISBN 0-688-09660-3 (lib. bdg.)
[1. Rhinoceros—Fiction.   2. Humorous stories.]
I. Kellogg, Steven, ill.   II. Title.
[PZ7.M462Ap   1990]
[E]—dc20   89-13803   CIP   AC

To Helen
S.K.
For Michael Baxter
M.M.

Appelard had a farm in Cyclone County, which has more hurricanes, cyclones, tornadoes, and thunderstorms than any county in the U.S.A.

On his farm he had a chicken, an old cow, a billy goat with one horn, and a fat old pig named Westminster.

But Appelard had no mule to pull his wagon or clear his land or plow his field. He had been too poor to buy another mule ever since his old mule blew away in the cyclone of '68.

In Loving Memory
OF
OLD MULE
WHO
BLEW AWAY
JULY 8 1968

Appelard's wagon lay on its side, unused. His fields were unplowed and covered with weeds. Sometimes Appelard would scratch his head and say, "Looks like I own a weed farm, doesn't it, Westminster?" All Westminster ever said was, "Grunt," except when he said, "Snort," and that was usually when a fly bothered him.

Appelard was so poor that he didn't even have a barn. The barn he had once had disappeared in the last tornado. That was the same storm that had sucked up the whole Z.P. Zanzibus circus train the day before the circus had been scheduled to open. It would've been the first circus ever to visit Cyclone County, and folks were terribly disappointed when Z.P. Zanzibus never showed up.

Appelard often said, "If that circus had actually opened here, I would've applied for a job on the circus train and gotten off this windy weed farm. But I wouldn't have left you animals behind. No siree. You're my best friends."

[3]

After the barn blew away Appelard didn't have the heart to let his animals sleep outside in the cold. So they all slept together in the creaky old one-room farmhouse.

Every night before going to bed Appelard said the same thing. "Someday when I save up enough money to buy us a mule, I'll plow them fields and grow the best crops you ever did see. Then we'll have enough money to go wherever we want."

Chicken would reply with a cackle, old cow would moo, billy goat would spit, and all Westminster did was grunt. None of them believed Appelard.

[4]

One night as they all slept curled up together in the big old bed, Appelard heard the sound of distant thunder. Then, some-time later, a loud noise came from the cellar.

"What's that?" said Appelard jumping up in bed and knock-ing Westminster to the floor. "Let's go see." So they all crept down to the cellar pushing the old cow ahead for protection.

Appelard couldn't believe his eyes! There in the root cellar eating mushrooms was the strangest looking creature he had ever seen. From its neck hung a tag which said:
BABY RHINOCEROS, PROPERTY OF CIRCUS.
Z.P. ZANZIBUS, INC., LTD.

"Why it's a little lost rhinosterwurst," said Appelard. "Poor little fellow must have been whirling around in that storm cloud ever since the last tornado. No wonder he's so hungry!"

Taking a mushroom from the mushroom bin Appelard led the baby rhinoceros out of the cellar and into the yard.

"You better sleep out here until we get better acquainted," he said, tying the rhinoceros to a big oak tree.

When they were all back in bed Appelard said, "Well, what shall we call him?"

"Moo," said the old cow.

"Pluck, pluck," said the chicken.

"Grunt," said Westminster, and all the billy goat did was spit.

"That doesn't help much," said Appelard. "I know, we'll call him Liverwurst. Liverwurst the rhinosterwurst."

Then they went to sleep.

The next morning Appelard and the animals awoke to another surprise. For there curled up at the foot of the bed slept Liverwurst.

"My goodness," said Appelard. "Just look at that." Sticking halfway through the door was the uprooted oak tree to which Liverwurst was still tied.

"That gives me an idea," said Appelard, jumping out of bed.

Appelard tied Liverwurst to the plow. With a big juicy mushroom dangling in front of Liverwurst's nose they plowed up all the weeds in the field.

With a heavy chain tied around Liverwurst, Appelard uprooted old tree stumps. Now they had new fields to grow even more crops in.

All spring long they worked the fields, with the old cow, the billy goat, the chicken, and Westminster the pig following along behind.

Each day crowds of people lined up along the roadside to watch.

"What in tarnation is that thing?" said one farmer to another. "Appelard's finally gone completely looney."

"I think it's called a Liverwurst," someone answered.

"That's not a Liverwurst," said someone else. "That's a Rhinosterwurst."

"You'd all be better off with one of those Rhinosterwursts," said Miss Rickets, the postmistress. "That thing plows better than a mule any day."

Fall came and soon all the trees were bare. It was time to harvest the crops. Everyone helped. There was even a bumper crop of mushrooms down in the root cellar. That pleased Liver-wurst, and he ate the whole bunch in one day.

"Well, it's time to go to market," said Appelard. He hitched Liverwurst to the creaky old wagon and piled it full of everything imaginable from potatoes to peanuts. Off to market they went with a mushroom held before Liverwurst's nose.

The town was filled with farmers from all over the

[14]

countryside. Even the mushroom farmers were there.

One little smell of all those fresh mushrooms was more than Liverwurst could stand. Straight through the marketplace he ran knocking over carts and baskets, spreading fruits and vegetables all over the ground. Before anyone could shout, "Stop eating those mushrooms!" he had already eaten two cartfuls.

Appelard tried to apologize to his neighbors. "I'm mighty sorry for what Liverwurst has done," he cried. "And I promise to pay for every bit of damage as soon as I sell my crops."

But the townspeople were furious.

Someone shouted, "Arrest that liverwurst rhinosterwurst whatchamacallit." And that's just what they did. They arrested Liverwurst. It took a big net and three horses just to drag him away.

"I can't very well put him in the dog pound," said the constable. "It's not big enough." So they put Liverwurst in the County Jail.

"Poor Liverwurst," said Appelard when he and the old cow, the billy goat, the chicken, and Westminster came to visit. "You didn't mean to do anything wrong." A big tear rolled down Liverwurst's cheek and fell on the cold stone floor of his cell.

Late that night Appelard and the animals shuffled slowly out of town and went home to their little one-room farmhouse. Appelard carried a big sack full of money from all the crops he had sold. But being rich wasn't any fun now that Liverwurst was in jail. They had planned a big celebration for that evening, but instead they just crawled sadly into the big old squeaky bed.

Large black storm clouds were forming around the moon, but Appelard and the animals didn't care. Each one silently shed a tear for Liverwurst before falling asleep.

Early the next morning they awoke to the sound of something stomping around on the front porch. A distant wind screamed, the house creaked, and all the windows rattled.

"Sounds like a tornado brewing," whispered Appelard.

"Moo," said the cow.

"Cackle pluck," said the chicken.

"Snort," said Westminster, and the billy goat spit.

Suddenly without warning the door crashed open, the wall cracked, the house shuddered and through the doorway stepped another rhinoceros. But this one wasn't small. It was big. Twice as big as Liverwurst.

"I have a feeling that this is Liverwurst's mother," said Appelard. "Let's run!"

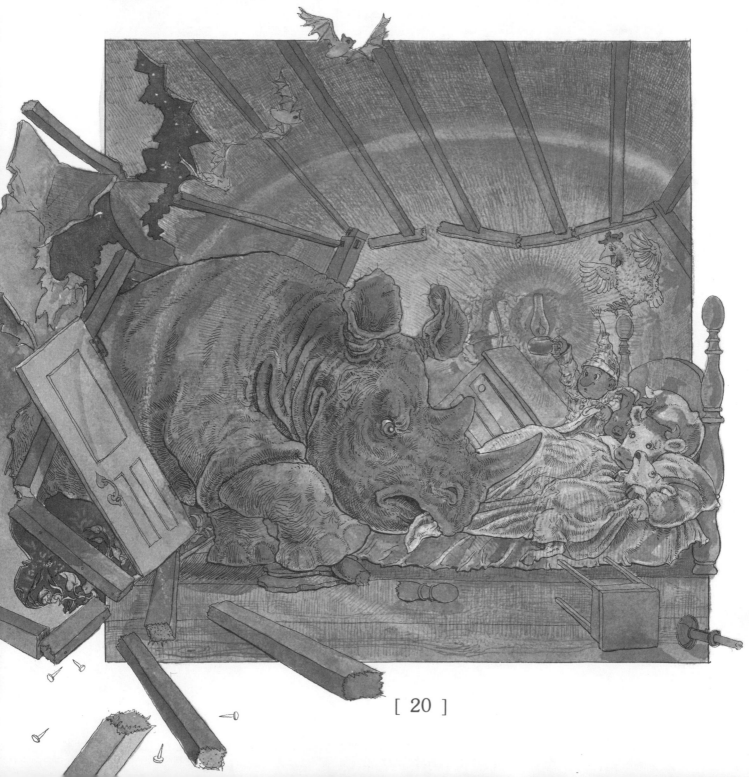

Through the window they jumped, even the old cow. Following close behind was Liverwurst's mother. She was much too big to jump through the window, so instead she knocked the wall down. The whole farmhouse collapsed.

"I knew that creaky old farmhouse was going to blow away or fall apart some day," said Appelard, "but I never thought a mother rhinosterwurst would knock it down." This time none of the animals made a sound. They were much too busy scrambling up the apple tree for safety.

Rhinoceroses don't have very good eyesight. Thinking everyone had just disappeared, Liverwurst's mother wandered off to town.

"Help!" cried the mayor.

"Call the police," said the constable.

"Oh, my goodness gracious me," said the scoutmaster. Down the main street of town walked Liverwurst's mother looking for Liverwurst. Straight to the jail she marched.

"Did you know," said the scoutmaster to the constable, "that rhinoceroses make sounds to signal each other just like us scouts?"

"I don't care!" hollered the constable. "Just look what that beast is doing to my new jailhouse." Right through the jailhouse wall plowed Liverwurst's mother.

Out the back of the jail ran the jailkeeper shouting, "It's the end of the world! Run for your life!"

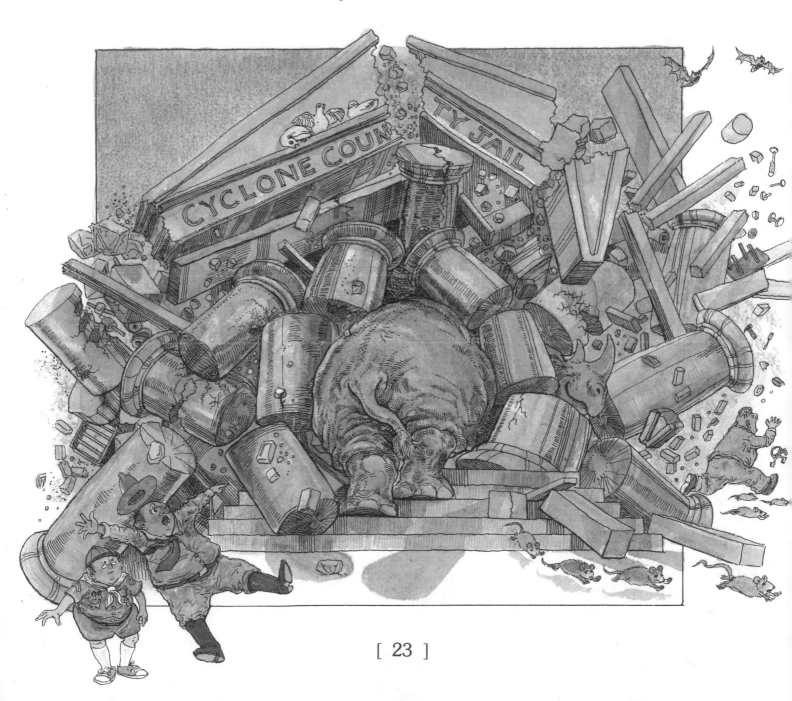

Liverwurst and his mother left the demolished jailhouse and headed down the road.

"It's all Appelard's fault!" shouted the townspeople. "Let's throw him out of town."

"He doesn't live in town," a little girl pointed out. "He lives in the country."

"Then he should be thrown out of the country!" said her mother, wagging a finger in the air.

"Form a posse!" bellowed the constable. "Appelard and his crazy critters have got to be stopped!" Every able-bodied person was made a deputy sheriff, and the old Civil War cannon was rolled out of the military museum.

Suddenly there was a terrible clap of thunder.

The storm that had been gathering the night before struck the town with a blinding downpour. The streets were flooded, the cannon sank out of sight in the mud, and the members of the posse stumbled home in confusion.

By the time the rain had stopped, Liverwurst and his mother were safely over the county line.

Along the road they met Appelard, the old cow, the billy goat, the chicken, and Westminster. They were happy to see Liverwurst, and even happier to see that his mother wasn't angry anymore.

"Mind if we all come with you and your mother?" asked Appelard. "Looks like we're not going to be too welcome around here." Liverwurst gave Appelard a big kiss on the cheek, then snorted a rhinoceros snort as if to say yes. Down the road they all walked together.

"I never did buy that mule, did I? But we finally have enough money to go wherever we want," said Appelard, holding up the sack of money.

Suddenly Appelard spotted a ragged figure lying in a nearby field. "Why, that poor fella must have been knocked flat by the storm," he said. "Let's stop and give him a hand."

To Appelard's surprise Liverwurst and his mother ran forward and began licking the fallen man's face. "Why, I recognize you from the circus poster!" cried Appelard. "You're Z.P. Zanzibus!"

The former ringmaster needed some rest after being battered by the tornado. Appelard took him to the next county and put him up at the best hotel.

During the weeks that Z.P. Zanzibus was recovering, Appelard visited him every day. The two became fast friends.

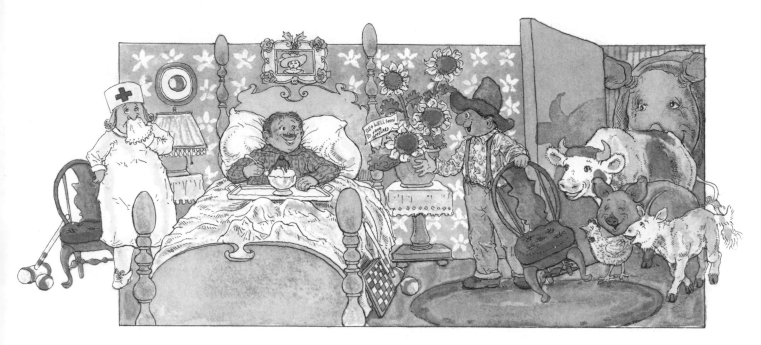

When Z.P. was on his feet again they agreed to be partners. They used the rest of Appelard's money to help buy a new circus train. Appelard was to be chief engineer.

They put notices in newspapers throughout the state.
Within a few weeks all the circus people who had been scattered
by the storm came back.

The circus was a great success wherever it went, and its

fame soon spread all the way across the country. Appelard loved his job as chief engineer.

But when the train wasn't rolling, he and Liverwurst spent most of their time in the caboose, which had been made into a comfortable home for the billy goat, the old cow, the chicken, and Westminster.